WHEN THUNDERS SPOKE

WHEN THUNDERS SPOKE

Virginia Driving Hawk Sneve

**illustrated by
Oren Lyons**

University of Nebraska Press
Lincoln and London

ED-P

First Bison Book printing: 1993
Most recent printing indicated by the last digit below:
10   9   8   7   6   5   4   3   2   1

Library of Congress Cataloging-in-Publication Data
Sneve, Virginia Driving Hawk.
When Thunders spoke / Virginia Driving Hawk; illustrated by Oren
Lyons.
p.   cm.
"Bison."
Summary: After a fifteen-year-old Sioux finds a sacred stick, unusual
things begin to happen to his family.
ISBN 0-8032-9220-1
1. Dakota Indians—Juvenile fiction.   [1. Dakota Indians—Fiction.
2. Indians of North America—Fiction.]   I. Lyons, Oren, ill.   II. Title.
PZ7.S679WH   1994
[Fic]—dc20
93-10953   CIP   AC

Reprinted by arrangements with Virginia Driving Hawk Sneve and
Holiday House

∞

For my Rock Hound Uncle, Harvey

TABLE OF CONTENTS

GLOSSARY OF SIOUX WORDS

ATE (*ah-tay*): father

COUP (*coo*): from the French meaning to strike or hit

HAN (*hunh*, the *a* has a nasal sound): yes

HOU (*how*): a greeting

OH HINH (*oh hee*): exclamation of shock, surprise or fear

TEHINDA (*tay-hin-dah*, the "h" is sounded as in the *ch* of the German "ach"): forbid, taboo

WAKALYAPI (*wah-call-yah-pee*): coffee

WAKAN (*wah-kanh*): holy

WAKANTANKA (*wah-kanh-tanh-kaw*): Great Spirit, God

WAŚTE (*wash-tay*): good

WHEN THUNDERS SPOKE

PROLOGUE

The barren, western prairies of the Dakota reservation are dotted with hills which abruptly rise from the surrounding ground. These isolated knolls of the northern plains are known as buttes. Some of them are really small mountains.

To the Plains Indians certain buttes were sacred places which the Great Spirit recognized. It was to one of these particular high hills that a young man would go in quest of a vision to guide his future life. Visions played an essential role in the religion of the Plains Indian. All young men were expected to leave the village and go alone to a butte to fast and pray until a vision came.

The Butte of the Thunders was known to the Sioux as a *Wakan*, a holy hill. They believed that the Thunders spoke from its flat top and that their message from *Wakantanka*, the Great Spirit, boomed across the plains. It was there the lightning struck and caused huge rocks that lay around the

butte's rim to break away, and only a determined, courageous young man could make the difficult ascent.

The Thunders favored a certain few of the vision seek-
ers, and to these young men special dreams came in which a
token of the Thunders' power was given.

Still, that was in the old time. Today the ways of the
past have been forgotten by many or contemptuously called
superstitions. Modern young men know little of the feeling
and spirituality of the old ones, and *Wakantanka* mourns.

Norman Two Bull, the third generation of his family to
live on the Dakota reservation, knew of the legends of the
Butte of Thunders, but that did not deter him from carelessly climbing among the rocks of the hill to gather agates.
The boy had been going to the butte for five years ever since
he was ten. It was then that his parents had first permitted
him to climb there, but only on the east side.

I

A DREAM COMMANDS

It was early evening. The sun hovered above the horizon, and the jutting hills and sparse wooden frame buildings of the Thunder Butte community cast long shadows. Norman hurried up the paved highway to the trading post. He knew Mr. Brannon would soon be locking the store for the night and the boy had to get there before it closed.

Sarah Two Bull, Norman's mother, was entertaining the newly organized church society of Indian women tonight and Norman was to exchange the agates he had collected for candy to serve the women. All morning Sarah had been in a frenzy of cleaning, ordering Norman about to fetch this or move that, until he had escaped to the solitude of the Thunder Butte. It was late afternoon when he returned. Sarah had scolded, fed the boy a quick supper, and sent him to the trading post.

Norman had been taking rough agates to Mr. Brannon

to trade for candy every summer for five years. He usually went during the day when trading was brisk. This evening the trading post, which was also the post office and only grocery store within twenty-five miles, was empty of customers.

The large front room of the building was dim in the fading sunlight. Norman hesitated in the open door when he saw that Mr. Brannon wasn't there but then walked slowly into the store. He looked around, taking advantage of the trader's absence to examine the wealth of merchandise.

Usually Norman obeyed the trader's strict law which forbade Indian children to go near the display counters in case they might be tempted to steal something. The counters and shelves were loaded with souvenir items of gaudy jewelry, child-size cowboy hats and headdresses, fancy tooled belts trimmed with shiny tin, wind-up toys and pretty colored stones. These trinkets were for the tourist children to buy and not for Indian boys and girls.

Norman moved slowly down an aisle between shelves stocked with canned goods. His mouth watered as he read the labels which made the contents sound so delicious. He wandered by the refrigerated meat case and his stomach growled yearningly as he saw the beef steaks and roasts invitingly displayed. 'Someday,' he thought, 'I'm going to have lots of money to buy all the food I want.'

He walked by the rack of shiny bright shovels, axes, pitch forks—tools that would make it a pleasure to do chores. He gave an envious sigh and moved on.

Norman stopped to look up at the guns hanging on a rack over a counter of hunting knives and hand guns. "Aah," he sighed. There was the rifle he longed to own. If only he had the courage to take it in his hands and examine it the way he had seen the white cowboys do. Norman wanted to touch the gun so much that without volition his hands slowly raised and he reached for the rifle.

Suddenly bright lights illuminated the room and a harsh voice commanded, "Stop!"

Norman, startled and blinking in the brightness, spun around on his heels and saw Mr. Brannon, his hand still on the light switch, standing by the door to the back room.

"What do you think you're doing?" the trader accused. "Trying to steal the rifle while I was out?"

"No-no," Norman stammered nervously. "No, Mr. Brannon. I wasn't going to steal it, honest." He glanced longingly back at the rifle. "I just wanted to look at it."

"Well, you do your looking without touching," the trader sneered. "What are you doing here this time of day anyway?"

Norman held out the old salt bag, half full of rocks. "Mom wants some candy for company tonight."

"Oh, got some more agates," Mr. Brannon said, taking the bag and dumping the rocks on the counter. "I'm glad you brought them, boy. I was running a little low and need more now that the tourists will be flocking in this summer. I was just loading the tumbler with the agates I had left—that's why I wasn't out here when you came in."

"Tumbler?" questioned Norman. "What's that?"

The trader laughed. "Boy, don't you know that I cut these rough agates into smaller sizes, put them in a tumbler that polishes them up. Tourists, especially kids, like to buy the smooth, pretty polished gem stones."

"You mean you sell agates to the tourists?" Norman asked in surprise.

"What did you think I did with them?" the man asked scornfully.

Norman shook his head. He felt foolish because he had never wondered what the trader did with his rocks. Then he became angry as he realized that the trader had been making money from the agates and gave Norman only candy in exchange.

"Why don't you give me money for the rocks I bring you?" Norman demanded and then looked at the floor, frightened by the audacity of his words.

But Mr. Brannon laughed. "No, boy. Don't you be getting big ideas. You've been happy with candy for five years and you know your mama likes sweets. Besides," the white man went on between chuckles, "those rough rocks ain't worth nothing until they're prettied up. You just keep bringing them to me and be glad I give you candy in exchange." He turned and filled a small paper sack with gum drops.

Norman felt trapped. He knew the trader was cheating him, but what could he do? If only he could polish the rocks himself, the boy thought, then he could sell directly to the tourists and not bother with Mr. Brannon!

"How much does one of those tumblers cost?" Norman asked and then took a step back as the trader exploded with laughter.

"Boy," said Mr. Brannon, "you're getting all kinds of uppity ideas, ain't you? That there lapidary equipment I got to cut and polish the stones cost me over one hundred dollars and I ordered it special from the city."

The trader stopped laughing and leaned over the counter so that his face was close to Norman's. "Don't you think

of going into competition with me, boy," he said in a low threatening voice.

Norman picked up the paper bag of candy and walked out of the trading post without answering. As he went down the steps he heard the trader laughing again. Stifled anger made the blood pound in the boy's ears and he broke into a run muttering, "I hate him! I hate him!" with each jolting stride.

Norman ran down the paved highway, past the gas station, the grade school and the few houses of the Thunder Butte community. He slowed to a walk at the end of two miles where he turned off onto the graveled road that went past his home.

In the gathering dusk the Thunder Butte loomed blue black, outlined by the yellow glow of the fading sun. The flickering flame from the light of the oil lamp in the Two Bull house seemed to be right at the base of the hill, but this was a deception of the failing day, for the butte was two miles to the west.

Norman's home was originally a one-room log cabin that had been erected in the early reservation days. Some time in the past, Norman didn't know when, a second room had been added and the house covered with siding, once painted white. As Norman approached his home he noticed the weathered shabbiness of the house, the sagging outhouse and horse shed, the dilapidated car parked in the yard, and his heart ached. He thought with anger of the trader's freshly painted, solidly constructed building. Although Norman had never seen it, he knew there was a comfortable apartment behind the store. The trader had indoor plumbing, central heating, and electricity, while Norman lived as the Two

Bulls had ever since coming to the reservation, surviving with no modern conveniences.

Norman's anger was replaced by sad frustration. The trader was probably one of the richest men on the reservation, Norman thought. Mr. Brannon's store was the only place for miles around where the Indians could trade. They had to come there even though they knew the trader's prices were too high. Many traded for essential commodities. They offered handcrafted leather work or beaded jewelry for food. When the pinch was very tight and they had nothing else left, some even parted with treasured heirlooms for groceries. Norman knew the trader sold these items for high prices, just as he did the polished agates.

Norman was glad that his father, John Two Bull, at least had a job. Many of the men were unemployed, and most Indian families were much poorer than the Two Bulls. John worked from sun up to dusk at the tribal ranch and still only made enough money to care for Norman and his mother. There would never be any extra to save to buy a rifle or lapidary equipment.

The boy saw the glow of a cigarette and knew his father sat smoking on the steps of the house. "Better hurry the candy in to your mom, Son," John said. "She's anxious to set it out before her ladies get here."

"Dad," Norman paused before going into the house, "does Mom know you're smoking?"

John Two Bull flipped the still burning cigarette butt onto the ground and mashed it under his heel. "Your mother won't allow smoking in the house, but she didn't say nothing about outside."

Norman smiled ruefully and asked, "Why did Mom

have to go and join that church for? Ever since she did all
she does is scold us. She isn't fun anymore."

John answered slowly, "Don't be too hard on her
Norman. She needs to have something now that you're not
little and needing her care all the time. Besides, the ladies of
the church do good. They make sure all the little kids have at
least one warm set of clothes to start school in."

"Oh, I know," Norman answered. "But it seems like
there ought to be more to it than that." He felt his father's
eyes on him.

"Like what?" John answered.

'What did I mean?' Norman wondered, his thoughts
confused by the anger and frustration he had just experi-
enced with the trader. Before he could answer, his mother
called from the house.

"Is that you, Norman? Bring the candy in right away."

"Better hurry," John said.

"What are we going to do while Mom has her meeting?" Norman asked as he started up the steps. "I don't want
to hang around here. Those women will grab us and start
preaching and praying over us about going to church."

John chuckled. "We'll walk over to Grandpa's. But you
get that candy into the house or you'll get a preaching from
your mom."

Norman took the candy to his mother. Sarah was standing before the mirror which hung over the washstand his
father had made from orange crates. She was combing her
long black hair. She wore a blue dress, carefully mended
nylon hose and high heels instead of her usual attire of jeans,
shirt and moccasins.

Norman watched her and suddenly noticed how small

she was. 'Why she only comes to my shoulder,' he thought with pleasure. His height was still a surprise to him.

"You look nice, Mom," he said, putting the candy on the table.

"Oh, Norman, what took you so long?" Sarah asked as she gave one last pat to her hair, which she'd tied back with a black ribbon. "This is my first time to have the ladies here and I want things to be nice. Do you think candy and coffee will be enough?" She took the paper bag from the table.

"I thought the ladies are coming to pray, not eat," Norman teased and then wished he hadn't spoken for Sarah began to scold.

"Norman, that is no way to talk. Our ladies do good work." She poured the candy into a bowl. "Oh, just gum drops. Didn't you ask Mr. Brannon if he couldn't give you chocolate mints just this once?"

"I forgot," Norman said. "But that old tightwad probably wouldn't have given them to me anyway. You know, Mom, that man is a no-good cheat."

"Norman, that's not a nice thing to say. Mr. Brannon is a faithful member of the church. He goes every Sunday, which is more than I can say for you and your father. And he puts five dollars in the collection every time."

"But, Mom!" Norman protested, shocked at his mother's defense of the trader, "he's been cheating me!"

Sarah waved her hand to silence the boy, "Norman, there isn't time to argue with you now. Bring that chair from your room out here. We might need it. I just don't know how many ladies will come. If it gets too crowded you and your Dad will have to stand."

"Don't worry about us," Norman said, carrying the

chair from the other room. "Dad and I are going over to Grandpa's while you have your meeting."

"Oh, I was hoping you would stay. The minister is coming later and he likes to visit with the men while the women have their meeting."

Norman headed for the door. "Sorry, but I better go see Grandpa. I ain't been over there for two days."

"Well, all right," Sarah reluctantly agreed. "But don't you smoke. I know that's what your father and Grandpa do. Sit and smoke and tell those heathenish stories of the old days."

"Heathenish?" Norman was surprised to hear his mother use such an unfamiliar word. "What do you mean by that?"

But Sarah waved him out of the house as she heard the sound of a car. "They're here. I think it's probably Mrs. White Lance driving, she was going to pick some of the other ladies up."

Norman escaped out the door and ran around to the back of the house. He followed his father, who had left as soon as the car drove into the yard.

It was dark now, but Norman and his father knew the well-worn path to Thunder Butte Creek. The boy's long legs matched his father's stride as he walked almost shoulder to shoulder with the man. Norman was nearly as tall as his father, but he was slender and did not yet have the breadth of shoulder and depth of chest that would come as he grew into manhood.

"Dad," Norman said as they walked in the starlit night. "What are we going to do about Mom? She acts like nobody does anything right anymore. All except Mr. Brannon," he said angrily, remembering Sarah's defense of the trader. "How can Mom think that old skinflint is any good?" He kicked at the weeds bordering the path. "Man, does he make me mad! You know, Dad, Mr. Brannon has been cheating me on those agates I bring him." Norman explained how the trader polished the stones with his lapidary equipment and then sold them to the tourists. "But he won't give me any money for the rocks I bring him. That isn't right, is it, Dad?"

John Two Bull sighed, "No, it isn't, Son. Old Joe Brannon's got a good thing going for him—and his father did too when he first opened that store years ago. There ain't a damn thing we can do about it."

"Well," Norman went on angrily, "I sure wish I could get some lapidary stuff and then I'd show that old tightwad! Only it costs about a hundred bucks," he finished lamely.

"I wish you could too, Norman," John said. "But don't count on it. A hundred dollars is half the money I make in a month."

They walked quietly on. Ahead, through the trees along the creek, they saw the flickering flames of a campfire and the dark shadow of Matt Two Bull's ridgepole tent.

"How come every summer when Grandpa comes to visit us he stays out here when he could stay in the house?" Norman asked. The boy had a deep affection for his grandfather, who often told him stories and taught him songs of the old days. It was Matt Two Bull who had shown Norman how to identify the agates and suggested the boy take them to the trader.

Norman's father laughed softly. "Grandpa says that he's

cooped up in a house all winter when he stays with your Aunt Martha."

They walked into the small clearing by the creek and saw the old man sitting erect, legs crossed, before the fire. Matt Two Bull lived with his daughter in the Dakota Agency town during the winter, but every summer he came to his old home on the reservation and pitched his ancient government issue tent. He stayed until the first snow and cold of winter forced him indoors.

The old man had turned more to the past as his years advanced. He had, despite Sarah's complaints, let his white hair grow long and wore it plaited in two braids which he wrapped with velvet strips. Over his red shirt he wore a fringed leather vest that he had fashioned from the skins of two deer John had shot. His daughter had colorfully decorated it with bead work. Black, shapeless store-bought trousers and beaded moccasins completed his costume. Norman knew that his mother thought Matt Two Bull was dirty because he seldom sent any of his clothes up to the house to be laundered, even though the old man greeted every day with a bath in the creek.

"*Hou!*" the old man said as Norman and his father seated themselves on the ground across the fire. "*Wakalyapi.*" He motioned to the chipped enameled coffee pot on the grate over the fire.

John poured the boiling brew into two tin cups that sat on a stump beside the fire pit. He reached over and refilled his father's cup. The two men and the boy sipped the hot coffee and stared into the dancing flames. Then Matt Two Bull spoke.

"I have had a strange dream. The same one for three nights. You know, Grandson," he said to Norman, "that when a dream comes to a man three times, it is a message that has been sent." He turned to look up at the butte, which loomed darkly behind him.

"Do you still go to the place of the Thunders to look for rocks?" he asked the boy.

Norman nodded and his grandfather went on. "Tomorrow you will go to search on the west side of the butte. You will carry a stout willow branch to probe for the rocks and as a weapon against the rattlesnakes." The old man paused and then added in a low tone, "You must go with caution."

"Was this your dream?" John asked.

Matt Two Bull nodded. "In my dream my grandson did this. I know that if he does as I tell him, the boy will cause some good thing to happen."

"But the west side of the butte is the place of the rock falls," John protested. "We have never let him go there. A slide could start and he might be injured."

Matt Two Bull shook his head. "In my dream he returned safely. But he must be careful." He looked across the fire, and the flickering light sharply etched the high cheek bones and sharp nose into protuberant nobility. His eyes were fathomlessly black and reflected the dancing flames.

Norman stared at his grandfather with wonder and fright. His thoughts raced. Matt Two Bull retained all of the old superstitions that the boy could not accept. Still he loved and respected his grandfather too much to refuse to do things in the traditional way when the old man urged him.

Besides, Norman had long wanted to explore the other

slopes of the butte, even to climb to the top, although his parents had forbidden him to do so. Now he would have a chance. For these reasons Norman heard himself say, "I'll go!" but his voice quavered and revealed the apprehension he felt.

"You are not afraid?" Matt Two Bull asked.

"No," Norman answered, trying to smile. "What is there to be afraid of?"

Matt Two Bull smiled and nodded. "You must ascend on the south side where the young men in the old time made a trail when they climbed the butte for their vision quest. You must be careful, for it is there that the Thunders sent rocks to fall and drove back the young men with little courage.

"When you have reached the top, you will descend on the west side. There is a special place to climb down, again made long ago. But the steps are broken, and on the west side the lightning which alerts us to the Thunders' message strikes and loosens the rocks so that there are many slides."

Norman nodded and his grandfather spoke no more of his dream. They talked of other things, but the old man seemed strangely preoccupied. It was getting late, and John and Norman rose to leave.

Matt Two Bull stood and walked to his tent and then returned with a diamond willow cane which had been carved and polished with care. One end was whittled into a sharp spear point.

"This willow branch came from the Thunder Butte Creek," Matt Two Bull said as he handed it to Norman. "I have had it for many years, but it is still strong and will help you in your search tomorrow."

Norman took the cane and looked fearfully at his grandfather. But the old man's face was now gentle and kind. "Take care," Matt Two Bull said in parting.

II

THUNDER BUTTE

The sun was just beginning to rise when John woke Norman the next morning.

"You must get an early start if you are going to go to the west side of the butte and return by supper," John said to the sleepy boy. "If you are not home by the time I get back from work, I'll come looking for you."

Norman reluctantly rose. Last night he had accepted his grandfather's command to go to the Thunder Butte without too many doubts. Yet now in the morning's chill light the boy wondered if his grandfather's dreams were the meaningless meanderings of an old mind, or if his grandather was really worthy of the tribe's respect as one of the few remaining wise elders who understood the ancient ways.

Norman dressed in his oldest clothes and pulled on worn and scuffed boots to protect his feet from the rocks and snakes of the butte. He heard his parents talking in the other

room and knew his father was telling his mother where
Norman was going.

As the boy entered the room, which was kitchen and
living room as well as his parents' bedroom, he heard his
mother say, "What if there is a rock slide and Norman is
hurt or buried on the butte? We won't know anything until
you get home from work, John. I don't want Norman to
go."

"The boy is old enough to have learned to be careful on
the butte. He'll be all right," John answered as he tried to
reassure Sarah. "Besides," he added, "my father dreamed of
this happening."

Sarah grunted scornfully, "No one believes in dreams or
in any of those old superstitious ways anymore."

"I'll be okay, Mom," Norman said as he sat down at the
table. "I should be able to find lots of agates on the west
side where there is all that loose rock. Maybe I can talk the
trader into giving me money for them after all." He spoke
bravely despite his own inner misgivings about going to the
butte.

Sarah protested no more. Norman looked at her, but
she lowered her head as she set a plate of pancakes in front
of him. He knew she was hiding the worry she felt for him.

John put on his hat and went to the door. "Don't forget
to take the willow branch with you," he said to Norman,
"and be careful."

Norman nodded and ate his breakfast. When he was
finished he stood up. "Guess I'll go," he said to his mother,
who was pouring hot water from the tea kettle into her dish
pan. When she didn't speak Norman took the willow cane

from where he had propped it by the door and his hat from the nail above it.

"Wait," Sarah called and handed him a paper bag. "Here is a lunch for you. You'll need something to eat since you'll be gone all day." She gave him an affectionate shove. "Oh, go on. I know you'll be all right. Like your dad said, you're old enough to be careful."

Norman smiled at his mother. "Thanks," he said as he tucked the lunch into his shirt. He checked his back pocket to see if he'd remembered the salt bag to put the agates in.

He walked briskly across the open prairie and turned to wave at his mother, who had come outside to watch him leave. She waved back and Norman quickened his pace. He whistled, trying to echo the meadowlarks who were greeting the day with their happy song. He swiped the willow cane at the bushy sage and practiced spearing the pear cactus that dotted his path. The early morning air was cool, but the sun soon warmed the back of his neck and he knew it would be a hot day.

He crossed the creek south of where Matt Two Bull's tent was pitched and then he was climbing the gentle beginning slope of the butte. He stopped and studied the way before him and wondered if it wouldn't be easier to reach the west side by walking around the base of the butte even though it would be longer. Then Norman smiled as he remembered his grandfather's command to climb the south trail that wound to the top. He decided to do what the old man wanted.

The ascent sharply steepened and the sun rose with him as Norman climbed. What looked like a smooth path from the prairie floor was rough rocky terrain. The trail spiraled up a sharp incline and Norman had to detour around fallen rocks. He paused to rest about half way up and then saw how sharply the overhanging ledge of the butte protruded. Getting to the top of it was going to be a difficult struggle. He climbed on. His foot slipped and his ankle twisted painfully. Small pebbles bounced down the slope and he saw a rattlesnake slither out of the way. He tightly clutched the willow branch and leaned panting against the butte. He sighed with relief as the snake crawled out of sight. He wiggled his foot until the pain left his ankle. Then he started to trudge up the incline again.

At last only the ledge of the butte loomed over him. There appeared to be no way up. Disgusted that his laborious climb seemed dead-ended he stubbornly tried to reach the top. Remembering the courage of the ancient young men who had struggled in this same place to gain the summit and seek their visions, he was determined not to go back. His fingers found tiny cracks to hold on to. The cane was cumbersome and in the way. He was tempted to drop it, but he thought of the snake he'd seen and struggled on with it awkwardly under his arm.

Finally Norman spied a narrow opening in the ledge which tapered down to only a few feet from where he clung. He inched his way up until he reached the base of the opening and then he found a use for the cane. He jammed the stout branch high into the boulders above him. Cautiously he pulled to see if it would hold his weight. It held. Using the cane as a lever he pulled himself to the top.

This final exertion winded the boy and he lay exhausted

on the summit, boots hanging over the edge. Cautiously he pulled his feet under him, stood and looked around.

He gazed at a new world. The sun bathed the eastern valley in pale yellow which was spotted with dark clumps of sage. The creek was a green and silver serpent winding its way to the southeast. His grandfather's tent was a white shoe box in its clearing, and beside it stood a diminutive form waving a red flag. It was Matt Two Bull signaling with his shirt, and Norman knew that his grandfather had been watching him climb. He waved his hat in reply and then walked to the outer edge of the butte.

The summit was not as smoothly flat as it looked from below. Norman stepped warily over the many cracks and holes that pitted the surface. He was elated that he had successfully made the difficult ascent, but now as he surveyed the butte top he had a sense of discomfort.

There were burn scars on the rough summit, and Norman wondered if these spots were where the lightning had struck, or were they evidence of ancient man-made fires? He remembered that this was a sacred place to the old ones and his uneasiness increased. He longed to be back on the secure level of the plains.

On the west edge he saw that the butte cast a sharp shadow below because the rim protruded as sharply as it had on the slope he'd climbed. Two flat rocks jutted up on either side of a narrow opening, and Norman saw shallow steps hewn into the space between. This must be the trail of which his grandfather had spoken.

Norman stepped down and then quickly turned to hug the butte face as the steps ended abruptly in space. The rest of the rocky staircase lay broken and crumbled below. The only way down was to jump.

He cautiously let go of the willow branch and watched how it landed and bounced against the rocks. He took a deep breath as if to draw courage from the air. He lowered himself so that he was hanging by his fingertips to the last rough step, closed his eyes and dropped.

The impact of his landing stung the soles of his feet. He stumbled and felt the cut of the sharp rocks against one knee as he struggled to retain his balance. He did not fall and finally stood upright breathing deeply until the wild pounding of his heart slowed. "Wow," he said softly as he looked back up at the ledge, "that must have been at least a twenty foot drop."

He picked up the willow branch and started walking slowly down the steep slope. The trail Matt Two Bull had told him about had been obliterated by years of falling rock. Loose shale and gravel shifted under Norman's feet, and he probed cautiously ahead with the cane to test the firmness of each step.

He soon found stones which he thought were agates. He identified them by spitting on each rock and rubbing the wet spot with his finger. The dull rock seemed to come alive! Variegated hues of brown and gray glowed as if polished. They were agates all right. Quickly he had his salt bag half full.

It was almost noon and his stomach growled. He stopped to rest against a large boulder and pulled out his lunch from his shirt. But his mouth was too dry to chew the cheese sandwich. He couldn't swallow without water.

Thirsty and hungry, Norman decided to go straight down the butte and head for home.

Walking more confidently as the slope leveled out he thrust the pointed cane carelessly into the ground. He suddenly fell as the cane went deep into the soft shale.

Norman slid several feet. Loose rocks rolled around him as he came to rest against a boulder. He lay still for a long time fearing that his tumble might cause a rock fall. But no thundering slide came, so he cautiously climbed back to where the tip of the willow branch protruded from the ground.

He was afraid that the cane may have plunged into a rattlesnake den. Carefully he pulled at the stout branch, wiggling it this way and that with one hand while he dug with the other. It came loose, sending a shower of rocks down the hill, and Norman saw that something else was sticking up in the hole he had uncovered.

Curious, and seeing no sign of snakes, he kept digging and soon found the tip of a leather-covered stick. Bits of leather and wood fell off in his hand as he gently pulled. The stick, almost as long as he was tall and curved on one end, emerged as he tugged. Holding it before him, his heart pounding with excitement, he realized that he had found a thing that once belonged to the old ones.

Norman shivered at the thought that he may have disturbed a grave, which was *tehinda*, forbidden. He cleared more dirt away but saw no bones nor other sign that this was a burial place. Quickly he picked up the stick and his willow cane and hurried down the hill. When he reached the bottom he discovered that in his fall the salt bag of agates had pulled loose from his belt. But he did not return to search for it. It would take most of the afternoon to travel around the base of the butte to the east side.

The creek was in the deep shade of the butte when he reached it and thirstily flopped down and drank. He crossed the shallow stream and walked to his grandfather's tent.

"You have been gone a long time," Matt Two Bull greeted as Norman walked into the clearing where the old man was seated.

"I have come from the west side of the butte, Grandpa," Norman said wearily. He sat down on the ground and examined a tear in his jeans and the bruise on his knee.

"Was it difficult?" the old man asked.

"Yes," Norman nodded. He told of the rough climb up the south slope, the jump down and finally of his fall which led him to discover the long leather-covered stick. He held the stick out to his grandfather who took it and examined it carefully.

"Are you sure there was no body in the place where you found this?"

Norman shook his head. "No, I found nothing else but the stick. Do you know what it is, Grandpa?"

"You have found a *coup* stick which belonged to the old ones."

"I know that it is old because the wood is brittle and the leather is peeling, but what is—was a *coup* stick?" Norman asked.

"In the days when the old ones roamed all of the plains," the old man swept his hand in a circle, "a courageous act of valor was thought to be more important than killing an enemy. When a warrior rode or ran up to his enemy, close enough to touch the man with a stick, without killing or being killed, the action was called *coup.*

"The French, the first white men in this part of the land, named this brave deed *coup.* In their language the word meant 'hit' or 'strike.' The special stick which was used to strike with came to be known as a *coup* stick.

"Some sticks were long like this one," Matt Two Bull held the stick upright. "Some were straight, and others had a curve on the end like the sheep herder's crook," he pointed to the curving end of the stick.

"The sticks were decorated with fur or painted leather strips. A warrior kept count of his *coups* by tying an eagle feather to the crook for each brave deed. See," he pointed to the staff end, "here is a remnant of a tie thong which must have once held a feather."

The old man and boy closely examined the *coup* stick. Matt Two Bull traced with his finger the faint zig zag design painted on the stick. "See," he said, "it is the thunderbolt."

"What does that mean?" Norman asked.

"The Thunders favored a certain few of the young men who sought their vision on the butte. The thunderbolt may have been part of a sacred dream sent as a token of the Thunders' favor. If this was so, the young man could use the thunderbolt symbol on his possessions."

"How do you suppose the stick came to be on the butte?" Norman asked.

His grandfather shook his head. "No one can say. Usually such a thing was buried with a dead warrior as were his weapons and other prized belongings."

"Is the *coup* stick what you dreamed about, Grandpa?"

"No. In my dream I only knew that you were to find a *Wakan*, a holy thing. But I did not know what it would be."

Norman laughed nervously. "What do you mean, *Wakan*? Is this stick haunted?"

Matt Two Bull smiled, "No, not like you mean in a fearful way. But in a sacred manner because it once had great meaning to the old ones."

"But why should I have been the one to find it?" Norman questioned.

His grandfather shrugged, "Perhaps to help you understand the ways—the values of the old ones."

"But nobody believes in that kind of thing anymore," Norman scoffed. "And even if people did, I couldn't run out and hit my enemy with the stick and get away with it." He smiled thinking of Mr. Brannon. "No one would think I was brave. I'd probably just get thrown in jail."

Suddenly Norman felt compelled to stop talking. In the distance he heard a gentle rumble which seemed to come from the butte. He glanced up at the hill looming high above and saw that it was capped with dark, low-hanging clouds.

Matt Two Bull looked too and smiled. "The Thunders are displeased with your thoughts," he said to Norman. "Listen to their message."

A sharp streak of lightning split the clouds and the thunder cracked and echoed over the plains.

Norman was frightened but he answered with bravado, "The message I get is that a storm is coming," but his voice betrayed him by quavering. "Maybe you'd better come home with me, Grandpa. Your tent will get soaked through if it rains hard."

"No," murmured Matt Two Bull, "no rain will come. It is just the Thunders speaking." There was another spark of lightning, and an explosive reverberation sounded as if in agreement with the old man.

Norman jumped to his feet. "Well, I'm going home. Mom will be worried because I'm late now." He turned to leave.

"Wait!" Matt Two Bull commanded. "Take the *coup* stick with you."

Norman backed away, "No, I don't want it. You can have it."

The old man rose swiftly despite the stiffness of his years and sternly held out the stick to the boy. "You found it. It belongs to you. Take it!"

Norman slowly reached out his hands and took the stick.

"Even if you think the old ways are only superstition and the stick no longer has meaning, it is all that remains of an old life and must be treated with respect." Matt Two Bull smiled at the boy. "Take it," he repeated gently, "and hang it in the house where it will not be handled."

Norman hurried home as fast as he could carrying the long stick in one hand and the willow cane in the other. He felt vaguely uneasy and somehow a little frightened. It was only when he reached the security of his home that he realized the thunder had stopped and there had been no storm.

"Mom," he called as he went into the house, "I'm home."

His mother was standing at the stove. "Oh, Norman," she greeted him smiling. "I'm glad you're back. I was beginning to worry." Her welcoming smile turned to a frown as she saw the *coup* stick in Norman's hand. "What is that?"

"Grandpa says it's a *coup* stick. Here," Norman handed it to her, "take a look at it. It's interesting the way it is made and decor—"

"No," Sarah interrupted and backed away from him. "I won't touch that heathen thing no matter what it is! Get it out of the house!"

"What?" Norman asked, surprised and puzzled. "There is nothing wrong with it. It's just an old stick I found up on the butte."

"I don't care," Sarah insisted. "I won't have such a thing in the house!"

"But, Mom," Norman protested, "it's not like we believe in those old ways the way Grandpa does."

But Sarah was adamant. "Take it out of the house!" she ordered, pointing to the door. "We'll talk about it when your dad gets home."

Reluctantly Norman took the *coup* stick outside and gently propped it against the house and sat on the steps to wait for his father. He was confused. First by his grandfather's reverent treatment of the *coup* stick as if it were a sacred object and then by Sarah's rejection of it as a heathen symbol.

He looked at the stick where it leaned against the wall and shook his head. So much fuss over a brittle, rotten length of wood. Even though he had gone through a lot of hard, even dangerous, effort to get it he was now tempted to heave it out on the trash pile.

Norman wearily leaned his head against the house. He suddenly felt tired and his knee ached. As he sat wearily rubbing the bruise John Two Bull rode the old mare into the yard. Norman got up and walked back to the shed to help unsaddle the horse.

John climbed stiffly out of the saddle. His faded blue work shirt and jeans were stained with perspiration and dirt. His boots were worn and scuffed.

"Hard day, Dad?" Norman asked.

"Yeah," John answered, slipping the bridle over the mare's head. "Rustlers got away with twenty steers last night. I spent the day counting head and mending fences. Whoever the thief was cut the fence, drove a truck right onto the range and loaded the cattle without being seen." He began rubbing the mare down as she munched the hay in her manger.

"How did your day on the butte go?" John asked.

"Rough," Norman answered. "I'm beat too. The climb up the butte was tough and coming down was bad too." He told his father all that had happened on the butte, winding up with the climax of his falling and finding the old *coup* stick.

John listened attentively and did not interrupt until Norman told of Matt Two Bull's reaction to the stick. "I think Grandpa's mind has gotten weak," Norman said. "He really believes that the *coup* stick has some sort of mysterious power and that the Thunders were talking."

"Don't make fun of your grandfather," John reprimanded, "or of the old ways he believes in."

"Okay, okay," Norman said quickly, not wanting another scolding. "But Mom is just the opposite from Grandpa," he went on. "She doesn't want the *coup* stick in the house. Says it's heathen."

He walked to the house and handed the stick to his

father. John examined it and then carried it into the house.

"John!" Sarah exclaimed as she saw her husband bring the stick into the room. "I told Norman, and I tell you, that I won't have that heathenish thing in the house!"

But John ignored her and propped the stick against the door while he pulled his tool box out from under the wash-stand to look for a hammer and nails.

"John," Sarah persisted, "did you hear me?"

"I heard," John answered quietly, but Norman knew his father was angry. "And I don't want to hear anymore."

Norman was surprised to hear his father speak in such a fashion. John was slow to anger, usually spoke quietly and tried to avoid conflict of any kind, but now he went on.

"This," he said holding the *coup* stick upright, "is a relic of our people's past glory when it was a good thing to be an Indian. It is a symbol of something that shall never be again."

Sarah gasped and stepped in front of her husband as he started to climb a chair to pound the nails in the wall above the window. "But that's what I mean," she said. "Those old ways were just superstition. They don't mean anything now —they can't because such a way of life can't be anymore. We don't need to have those old symbols of heathen ways hanging in the house!" She grabbed at the *coup* stick, but John jerked it out of her reach.

"Don't touch it!" he shouted and Sarah fell back against the table in shocked surprise. Norman took a step forward as if to protect his mother. The boy had never seen his father so angry.

John shook his head as if to clear it. "Sarah, I'm sorry. I didn't mean to yell. It's just that the old ones would not per-mit a woman to touch such a thing as this." He handed

Norman the stick to hold while he hammered the nails in the wall. Then he hung the stick above the window.

"Sarah," he said as he put the tools away, "think of the stick as an object that could be in a museum, a part of history. It's not like we were going to fall down on our knees and pray to it." His voice was light and teasing as he tried to make peace.

But Sarah stood stiffly at the stove preparing supper and would not answer. Norman felt sick. His appetite was gone. When his mother set a plate of food before him he excused himself saying, "I guess I'm too tired to eat," and went to his room.

But after he had undressed and crawled into bed he couldn't sleep. His mind whirled with the angry words his parents had spoken. They had never argued in such a way before. "I wish I had never brought that old stick home," he whispered and then pulled the pillow over his head to shut out the sound of the low rumble of thunder that came from the west.

III

THE CHANGE

Norman slept late the next morning. He did not hear his father leave and his mother, knowing how weary he was, did not call him. After he got up and had his breakfast he decided to return to the butte to look for the lost bag of agates.

"Mom," he said to Sarah, who was sweeping the floor of the small room, "do we have any heavy rope around the place?"

"There may be some out in the shed," Sarah answered. "What do you need it for?"

"I'm going back up to the butte to look for my agates. I'm going to climb it again, and I think a rope will make it easier."

"Oh, Norman, I wish you wouldn't," Sarah said worriedly.

"Don't fuss, Mom," Norman laughed. "I won't bring home any more old things."

Sarah shrugged, and Norman could see that she was still angry about the *coup* stick. "That's not the only reason I don't want you to go," she said. "You could get hurt climbing that rough place, and there are rattlesnakes too."

But Norman wasn't listening. He was staring at the *coup* stick above the window. Was he imagining things, or was the leather covering on the stick more supple and somehow not so old?

"Mom, did you clean the stick?"

"Umph," Sarah snorted. "You know I'm not supposed to touch the old thing. Why?" Then she looked up at the stick and gasped.

"It looks different, doesn't it?" Norman said.

His mother nodded, eyes wide with fright. "Norman, take it down. Take it back to the butte and bury it again."

Norman felt his mother's fear but shook it off as he grabbed his hat from the hook by the door. "Oh, Mom," he laughed nervously.

"I mean it, Norman. Take it out of here before something bad happens to us. I'm scared."

Norman laughed again. "Mom, now you're being more superstitious than Grandpa. The stick just looks different in the daylight. That's all. It's harmless." He left the house before his mother could protest more.

Norman found a coil of rope in the shed and hung it over his shoulder. He took the willow cane and set off for the butte. He refused to think of the *coup* stick. He wasn't going to let his mother's fears upset him.

He used the rope to pull himself up the butte and to lower himself down the other side. With the rope he had no difficulty and was soon walking down the west slope. He found the salt bag lying right in his path. As he reached for it he heard the staccato whirring click of a rattlesnake nearby. He froze and then slowly stood and looked around. He saw the snake, coiled, ready to strike, and without thought Norman thrust the pointed end of the willow cane at the serpent. He speared the rattler at the base of its skull, but it was still alive and dangerous. Again and again Norman stabbed until the snake's writhings ceased and it was still.

He left the dead rattler, picked up the salt bag and quickly had it filled with agates. He wished he had brought a larger bag, for the rocks were plentiful and easy to find. Some of the agates were too big to fit in the salt bag, which he had tied to his belt. So he carried one large rock in his hand to show it to his grandfather.

He went back to the dead snake and saw that the ants and flies had already gathered on its mangled head. He tied the rattler in the rope and set off down the hill. He moved awkwardly down the slope with the snake and rope swinging against his back, the heavy bag of rocks bumping clumsily against his thigh, the cane in his right hand and the big agate in the other. He was ready to rest when he reached his grandfather's camp.

"*Hou,*" Matt Two Bull greeted as Norman walked into the clearing. "Have you been up the butte again?"

Norman nodded as he lowered the large agate and cane to the ground. "I went back to get my agate bag, which I lost yesterday. When I found it, I found this." He held out the rattlesnake, and as it dangled limply in his hands the boy realized that it was almost four feet long. His face paled and he felt sick to his stomach.

Matt Two Bull went quickly to Norman and took the

snake. "Did its fangs strike you?" he asked, concerned at the boy's pallor.

Norman shook his head and tried to smile. "No," he replied, embarrassed by his weakness. "I just realized how big a snake it was and well—I guess I didn't have time to be scared when I killed it. But—now—golly, I get weak in the knees thinking what could've happened if I'd missed when I was spearing that rattler."

The old man chuckled. "The willow cane I made for you is a good weapon."

"It sure is," Norman agreed. "You know, Grandpa, I've seen lots of rattlers on the butte, but this is the first one I've ever killed." Pride was in his voice now as he looked at the snake his grandfather held.

"Killing the snake was a brave thing," Matt Two Bull said. "It must be a grandpa snake—it is about as big as most rattlers get. Are you going to take it home?"

"Oh, no!" Norman exclaimed. "Mom would never let me go back to the butte if she saw the snake. I was hoping you'd show me how to skin it. I thought it would make a nice belt."

Matt Two Bull nodded. He squatted down on the ground, pulled his knife from the sheath at his belt and began to skin the snake.

Norman sat cross-legged beside his grandfather and watched. "Nope," he said shaking his head. "Mom wouldn't like it at all if she knew I killed a rattler. She's getting so fussy over so many things. You should have heard her carry on about the *coup* stick last night." Norman told his grandfather about Sarah's opposition to having the stick in the house.

"Then this morning," Norman went on as his grandfather tacked the green hide to a board so that it wouldn't curl as it dried, "Mom was all upset again. The stick looked different somehow—not so old and rotten. I told her that it only looked different because it was daylight."

Matt Two Bull was finished with the snake. He made no response to Norman as he carried the skinned carcass to the creek bank. "We will leave the snake here for my friend the owl who lives nearby. He will be glad to have the fresh meat." The old man washed his hands in the creek and motioned for Norman to do the same. "We must be sure there is none of the rattler's poison on our skins."

"It is getting late," the old man said as they rose from the creek. "I will come to your house for supper tonight and to see the coup stick."

Norman picked up his willow cane and then the big agate, which he handed to his grandfather. "Oh, yes, Grandpa," he said, "I almost forgot about this big agate I found. There are lots more big ones on the west slope. Have you ever seen one so big?"

Matt Two Bull examined the agate and then nodded. "I've seen big ones, but not since I walked the butte as a young man. Then I didn't know what they were." He handed it back to Norman. "Take it to the trader, I bet he will give you money for it."

The sun was beginning to set behind the butte when Norman and his grandfather reached the house. They waited as they saw Norman's father ride into the yard.

"*Hou, Ate,*" John greeted his father. "How'd you know we were having steaks for supper, Dad?" he asked smiling.

"Leave it to an old Indian to smell good meat even before it's cooked!" He reined the mare in front of them.

"Here, Son," he said to Norman, handing the boy a large paper-wrapped package. "Take this hunk of beef in to your mom. We're going to feast tonight!"

Norman took the meat. "What did you do?" he asked in surprise, "butcher one of the tribe's steers?" He was half teasing as he referred to the poaching of the herd that was sometimes done by hungry Indians.

"That's just what I did," John laughed and then seeing the dismay on Norman's face added, "Don't worry. It's all legal. Take the meat into the house. I'll tell you about it after I put the mare up."

Sarah was pleased with the meat but also suspicious of how John had obtained it. "He didn't steal it, did he, Norman?" she asked worriedly. "We're not so hard up that he has to do that."

John walked into the house as she spoke. "It's okay, Sarah. Just cook the meat. Dad's here for supper and he ain't had a good steak in a long time."

The Two Bulls loved good beef as did all of the Sioux. In the old days they had been free to hunt the buffalo, and its rich sweet meat was a staple of their diet. But the buffalo herds were gone, and now when there was money to buy meat it was included at every meal. Rarely did the Two Bulls have as much meat as was on the table tonight and they ate their fill. It was tough, but the flavor was good and they relished every succulent bite while John told how he had acquired the beef.

"One of the other hands was out riding fence and found

this steer that somehow had broken loose all tangled in the barbed wire. The poor critter was cut up so bad that we had to kill it. We butchered it and Jason Lance, the foreman, took the biggest share into town for the old folks' home—so he said," John added scornfully. "But I wouldn't be surprised if he just took the meat to his own old home. The rest of us each got about the size chunk I brought home."

After supper Norman and his father walked Matt Two Bull back to his tent while Sarah washed the dishes.

Norman felt good. His stomach was pleasantly full and he was happy that his parents had not quarreled as they had the evening before. Remembering the *coup* stick he spoke to his grandfather, who was walking ahead with John.

"Grandpa?" Norman asked. "Did you think to look at the *coup* stick while you were eating?"

They had arrived at the camp, and the old man answered, "*Han*," while he busied himself lighting his lantern.

"What's wrong with the stick?" John asked.

"It's sort of changed," Norman explained. "Mom and I noticed it this morning and she got all upset. I thought maybe it just looked different in the daylight. Did you notice anything, Grandpa? I forgot to look."

Matt Two Bull nodded, but said nothing.

"But, why?" Norman questioned. "Why is it changing?"

But the old man didn't answer. He turned to look up at the dark wall of the butte behind him and Norman shivered with apprehension. Then his grandfather turned back to his grandson as if he sensed the boy's discomfort. "Don't be afraid. Remember that the *coup* stick is *Wakan*. Only good

will come." He went into his tent, and Norman and h.
father walked home.

After they entered the house John and Norman stood
looking up at the *coup* stick.

"See, Dad," Norman whispered excitedly. "It's changed
—even more than it was this morning."

Sarah looked up from where she sat at the table. *"Oh
hinh!"* she gasped. The Sioux expression of wonder and surprise sounded strange coming from her because she always
spoke English.

Now, not only did the leather on the stick appear
fresher but the faded red and yellow colors of the thunder·
bolt design glowed brightly in the dim light of the oil lamp.
The design seemed newly painted.

"You haven't touched it?" John asked Norman and
Sarah, who shook their heads. "And I haven't," he added
softly.

"John," Sarah said recovering from her shock, "take
that thing out of the house. It's not good. Something bad is
going to happen."

But John shook his head, "No, Sarah. Nothing bad will
happen. Dad says the stick is *Wakan*. Don't be afraid of it."

"I'm not afraid," Sarah protested, but Norman heard the
fear in her voice, "but it just doesn't make sense."

John shrugged and turned away from the stick. "There
is nothing to worry about and the stick is going to stay
here." He yawned and walked to the bed in the corner. "It's
late. Let's get some sleep."

Norman went to bed and was glad not to be sleeping in
the same room with the *coup* stick. He wished he could

calmly accept the changes in the stick as his father and grandfather did. He shared his mother's fear but also wished she were more tolerant of how the men felt.

Despite his confused thoughts Norman fell asleep. His dreams were a mad swirl. He was chasing Mr. Brannon with the *coup* stick, and just as Norman was about to strike, the man turned into a rattlesnake and the thunder roared.

Norman woke in alarm, breathing hard, with his blanket tangled about him. He smoothed out the bedding and then lay quietly listening. He heard the low rumble of thunder in the west and was somehow comforted by knowing he hadn't dreamed the sound.

IV

GOOD FORTUNE

Norman heard his father leave the next morning, but drowsily stayed in bed. It was too early to be up, he thought, and then he remembered the agates he had collected yesterday. Norman rose and dressed. He would take the bag to Mr. Brannon and again try to talk the trader into paying money for them.

"If Mr. Brannon won't pay me for the agates," Norman said to his mother while he ate his breakfast, "I just ain't going to give them to him. I'm his best supplier of the rocks and when he runs short—then I bet he'll pay me!"

"Well, maybe so, Norman," Sarah said as she cleared the table. "But a little candy now and then is nice to have."

Norman snorted disgustedly at his mother. "I could buy lots of candy if I had money," he said, rising from the table. He picked up the agates and put on his hat.

Wait, Norman," Sarah said, getting her purse from the
er by the bed. "I'll give you a ride to the trading post.
going over to the church. My guild is going to clean it
day." Then she glanced nervously at the stick. "And I
don't want to stay here alone with that thing any more than
I have to."

Norman looked at the stick. The changes he had noted
the night before were even more evident in the morning
light. He felt a return of his unease.

"I wish you would take it away, Norman," Sarah said.
"I know something bad is going to happen even if your
father doesn't think so."

"Aah, Mom," Norman said teasingly. "You were
worried yesterday too and we had a good feast last night."

"Well, I still don't like it," Sarah said as they left the
house.

"Let me drive, Mom," Norman asked, hoping to take his
mother's mind off the *coup* stick. "I haven't had much of a
chance to drive since I took Driver's Ed. in school."

"Okay," Sarah said, handing Norman the ignition key
as they climbed into the car. "Remember you got to choke it
good or it won't start."

Norman drove the car to the trading post, where he got
out, and Sarah slid over into the driver's seat. "I'll be home
for dinner, Norman," she said as she drove off.

The trading post was filled with tourists, so Norman sat
on the porch steps and waited. He could hear Mr. Brannon
talking in pleasing, placating tones to the people inside.
'Those tourists must be buying a lot of stuff,' he thought as
he listened. 'That old skinflint only talks nice to people who
have money. He never talks to Indians that way.'

Two little white boys ran noisily out of the store, pily beating on tin tom toms, the kind of cheap fake sounirs the white people always bought, thinking they wer getting something "authentic." The two white children were followed by a tall white man who was complaining to the woman at his side.

"I was hoping I could find some rough agates. I'd rather cut and polish my own stones. I thought sure there'd be some for sale here. This seems like good country for finding agates."

Norman, usually shy of strangers and especially of white people, jumped up without thinking. "I have rough agates for sale," he said loudly.

The man stopped and Norman held out the salt bag. The tourist poured a few of the rocks in his hand and nodded. "These look like good ones. How much do you want for them?"

Norman was shy again. He looked down at his boot, which was nervously kicking the step. "Don't know," he muttered. "Never sold any before."

The white man and woman laughed. "Well, what were you going to do with these?" the man asked.

"Take them to him." Norman jerked his head toward the trading post and to his horror saw Mr. Brannon glaring at him through the door.

"Well, how much does the trader give you for the rocks?" the tourist asked.

"Candy," Norman muttered and looked down again at his kicking boot.

"Candy?" The white man was surprised. "You mean you want candy in exchange?"

"N—no," Norman stammered nervously, wishing he
n't feel so tongue-tied. He was tempted to take the bag
ck and run for home. "I'd just as soon have money."

"Well," the man pondered, looking again at the agates,
"there seem to be good stones here. How would two dollars
be?"

Norman was pleased with the amount offered, but he
could only gulp, swallow and nod his head. He couldn't
speak even to say thank you when the man held out two
dollar bills. Norman took them and stuffed the money in his
jeans' pocket. He watched the tourists get in their car and
managed a jerky wave as they drove away.

"What are you trying to do, boy?" The trader's angry
voice brought Norman out of his bemused stupor.

"Wh—what do you mean?" Norman asked in bewilder-
ment.

"You know what I mean," Mr. Brannon said nastily.
"Selling those rough agates to that tourist when you're supposed to give them to me!"

Norman no longer felt shy and tongue-tied. He was
angry. He drew himself up to his full height and glared down
at the fuming short man.

"I can sell the rocks to whoever I want to," he said
loudly. "And there's nothing you can do about it." He turned
to leave.

"Now, just a minute, boy." Mr. Brannon rushed down
the steps and grabbed Norman's arm.

Norman shook off the trader's grasp and turned furi-
ously on the man. "My name ain't 'boy,'" he growled. "It's
Two Bull—and don't you ever touch me again!"

To Norman's surprise the trader backed off. "Now,

don't get all excited, boy—er, I mean, Two Bull," Mr. Bra
non whined. "I forgot that you ain't a little kid no more.
just wanted to say that I'll buy your rocks from you."

Norman almost laughed aloud at the trader's pleading
manner, but he made his face stern and his voice deep as he
asked, "Two dollars a bag?"

The trader began to look angry again, but nodded yes.

"And how much for rocks like this?" Norman asked,
holding out the larger agate he had kept in his hand.

Mr. Brannon let out his breath and took the agate. "This
is one of the biggest I've seen around here," he said excitedly. "Did you find it on the butte?"

Norman nodded.

"Are there a lot of big ones up there?"

"Yeah," Norman answered. "Next time I go up there
I'm going to have to take a bigger bag to bring the rocks
down in."

"I got gunny sacks you can use," Mr. Brannon offered.
"But you aren't going to be able to carry many of this size
in a sack—it'll be a heavy load."

Norman reached over and took the agate back from Mr.
Brannon. "How much you going to give me for big agates
like this? I'll figure out a way to haul them down if the
price is right."

Mr. Brannon cleared his throat and hummed a little as if
he were thinking. "Well, now," he finally said, "you understand I can't really tell how good the agates will be until I
cut into them. How's twenty-five to fifty cents—depending
on the quality, of course."

Norman hesitated. He had no idea of the value of the
agates, and Mr. Brannon could easily cheat him again. Still,

o dollars for a salt bag full of small agates and at least a quarter for a larger rock would be more money than Norman had ever had. He nodded his agreement.

Mr. Brannon gave Norman a gunny sack and waved as Norman walked away. Norman strode tall, feeling as dignified and important as the richest man in the world. When he knew he was out of sight of the trading post he let out a joyful whoop and ran the rest of the way home.

When his mother returned from the church Norman happily told her what had happened and gave her the two dollar bills. "Put the money away for me, Mom. I'm going to get more and then I'll buy me that rifle so that I can go deer hunting this fall. Then I'll get me that lapidary stuff and to hell with Skinflint Brannon!"

"Norman!" Sarah scolded. "That's enough of that kind of language and don't talk bad about Mr. Brannon. Besides," she cautioned, "it'll take a lot of money to get all the things you want."

"I'll get it," Norman promised. "I'm going to the butte now and bring home a bushel of rocks!"

On the butte Norman filled the small salt bag, which he tied to his belt, and then searched for larger agates. He found six, which he put in the gunny sack, and then set off for home. The rocks were heavy and he was tired when he got back to the house. That evening he was proud to tell his father how he had gotten money from the trader.

John smiled at Norman's cheerfulness. "I bet Joe Brannon is upset about having to pay hard cash for once."

Sarah sniffed in disapproval at the way Norman and his father were talking about the trader, but she said nothing.

"I have good news too," John said.

"More meat?" Norman asked jokingly.

"Not right now," John said. "But we'll be able to h[e]
more meat on the table from now on. I got promoted [t]
ranch foreman today."

"Oh," breathed Sarah, "how did that happen?"

"You remember yesterday I told you that Jason had
said he was taking most of the beef we butchered to the old
folks' home and how I suspected that he had done no such
thing but was taking it to his own house? Well, he did
worse than that. Mr. Walking, the tribal police chief, caught
Jason selling the beef to the Indians—and that was the end
of his being foreman."

"And you got the job!" Norman let out a joyful
whoop. "Yippee! That means we'll have more money, won't
it, Dad?" His father nodded, and Norman went on, "Now
I'll get my rifle and tumbler for sure!" He let out another
wild yell.

"Don't get all carried away with your big plans, Son,"
John cautioned. "I'll only be getting twenty dollars a week
more. We ain't going to get rich very fast on that."

"Well, our luck sure has turned good, hasn't it?" Norman said. "Why do you suppose that is?"

"It's God's will," Sarah murmured.

"You know what I think," Norman said half teasing. "I
think it's because of the *coup* stick." He got up and walked
to where the stick was hanging. "Since it has been up there it
has changed and with each change something good has happened to us."

"I think you're right, Son," John said, standing beside
Norman.

"Mom," Norman turned to his mother, who still sat at

table, her mouth in a tight line that expressed her disap-
oval, "you must see that there's something special about
ne stick. You've seen the changes and the good things that
have happened. You can't think it's bad now."

There was a knock on the door and Sarah jumped up to
open it. "It's the minister," she said.

Norman looked curiously at his father for an explana-
tion. But John was surprised too. Usually Sarah told them
when the minister was coming to visit and there was a mad
rush to tidy up the house, with Sarah scolding father and
son until she felt the house was presentable. But tonight the
supper dishes were still on the table and she made no fuss.

"Come in, Reverend Parks," Sarah greeted the tall thin
white man in his drab black suit. The minister removed his
proper black hat as he entered the room.

"Good evening, Mrs. Two Bull," the minister replied,
"Mr. Two Bull, Norman." He shook hands with everyone.

"We're just finishing our supper. Would you like some
coffee?" Sarah spoke nervously as she cleared a place at the
table.

"That would be good," Reverend Parks answered.

Norman sat on the bed in the dark corner of the room
where he could watch the minister and his father, who sat at
the table.

"Congratulations," Reverend Parks said to John. "I understand that you've been promoted to ranch foreman. I'm
sure you'll do a good job."

John nodded his thanks but said nothing.

"Good weather we've been having," the minister said,
sipping his coffee. "It must make your work out-of-doors
more pleasant."

"We never get enough rain around here in the s[ummer]," John answered. "We could use a good soaking no[w,] water holes are about dry and the grass is burning up [no] good for grazing."

The minister, who was new to the plains, was unco[n-] cerned by his lack of knowledge of the area. "Well, the[n,] we'll have to pray for rain," he said smiling.

John nodded again.

The minister cleared his throat and pushed the empty cup away from him. "I understand from Mrs. Two Bull," he said, "that you have recently acquired an old relic of historic interest."

John shot a glance at Sarah, who jumped up to get the coffee pot. Norman guessed that his mother had asked the minister to come.

John nodded and motioned to where the *coup* stick hung over the window. Reverend Parks got up to look at it. He reached up to touch it, but John stood and said, "No."

The minister turned in surprise, "Can't I examine it?"

John shook his head. "It is very old and brittle with age. The less it is handled the longer it will last."

"It doesn't look very old," the minister said.

"But it is," Sarah spoke. "We were just talking, before you came, of the strange way the stick has changed—become newer since it's been up there. I—I don't like it," she added nervously. "I was hoping Reverend Parks could talk some sense into you and Norman," she said to John, "so that you'd get rid of that stick."

"I've told you before," John said gently to Sarah, "there's nothing to be afraid of. The *coup* stick is *Wakan* and only good will happen while it is here."

akan," the minister mused, "that means holy, and the
a name for God is *Wakantanka*."

"Yes," John agreed. "The white missionaries called their
d *Wakantanka*, which is our name for the Great Spirit."

"Then," Norman suddenly said from his corner, "*God*
and *Wakantanka* must be the same thing."

"No," the minister shook his head sadly. "One is Christian and the other is—is . . ." He stumbled for words, and
Norman thought the man was trying not to offend.

"Heathen?" John finished for the minister. "But the
Great Spirit is everywhere as you believe God is."

"True," answered the minister, "but your people worshipped the sun, the winds, the earth—"

"But such things only represented *Wakantanka*. Don't
you have such symbols of God in your church?" John said
and then shook his head. "I can't explain this very well. You
should talk to my father. He can tell it better than I can."

"I have tried to talk to your father," the minister said
sternly. "But every time I go to his tent he is not there. I
don't think we wants to talk to me."

"That's because he's afraid you'll make him cut his hair
and go to church," John smiled. "My father believes he can
pray best out-of-doors, directly to *Wakantanka*."

"I understand your father believes that the thunder lives
on the butte?" the minister asked.

"Maybe it does," Norman spoke again. "When it thunders the sound seems to come from the butte."

Reverend Parks smiled at Norman. "Is the butte where
you found—" he waved his hand to the *coup* stick.

Norman nodded.

"What purpose did it once have? Was it used ship?"

"No," John answered and explained the use of the stick. "Only brave warriors had one," he finished.

The minister sat quietly looking at the stick. He ro. and said, "A very curious and valiant life your people used to live." The man raised his hand. "A prayer before I leave you," he said, bowing his head.

Sarah lowered her head and closed her eyes. John stared straight ahead, and Norman looked at the *coup* stick.

'What did the minister mean by curious?' Norman won- dred. Did the man think the Indians were freaks? Anger and sadness filled the boy's heart at the minister's lack of under- standing. Norman did not hear the prayer.

V

HONOR THE OLD WAYS

Norman rose early the next morning and was at the breakfast table before his father left for work.

"What are you going to do today, Son?" John asked.

"I'm going to take the agates I found yesterday to the trader this morning and then go on back to the butte to get more."

"Before you go, I think you should run on over to Grandpa's and let him know that the minister might be out to see him. If Grandpa doesn't know about him coming, he'll probably hide someplace and not talk to the minister again. Tell Grandpa that I think he should talk to the minister. Grandpa can explain the old religion better than anyone and maybe change some of the crazy ideas that minister has about Indians."

Sarah sniffed scornfully, "I suppose you think Grandpa will talk Reverend Parks into thinking those old ways were Christian."

"Well, at least someone should let the preacher ⸺ that the old ways weren't bad," John said as he rose to le⸺ "Think you'll have time to go over to Grandpa's before y⸺ go to the trading post?" he asked Norman.

Norman said he would and left the house soon after his father did. Sarah called after the boy, "Tell Grandpa to send his dirty clothes back with you. I'm going to drive over to the laundromat at the agency to wash this afternoon and I might as well do Grandpa's clothes too."

Norman walked quickly to the tent on the creek. He found his grandfather rinsing his breakfast dishes in the stream. Norman smiled as he thought of how his mother would disapprove.

"Hey, Grandpa," Norman called, "you're supposed to wash your dishes with hot water and soap."

Matt Two Bull grunted in disgust. "While your grandmother was alive, she always said such things about washing. She got fussy like a white woman after a government health lady came to the reservation and gave housekeeping lessons. Everything had to be washed with soap. Your grandmother even tried to make me bathe with it."

"Did you?" Norman asked.

"Hah," snorted the old man, "not white man's soap! Indian soap from the yucca plant gets me clean."

"Well," Norman laughed, "Mom wants you to send your dirty clothes over so she can wash them this afternoon."

"My clothes ain't dirty yet," Matt Two Bull said as he set his plate, cup and frying pan on the stump to air dry. "I wash my body every day and don't do hard sweaty work. There's nothing to get my clothes dirty."

Norman laughed again, wishing that he could say the
same thing to his mother. She was always making him change
into clean clothes.

"Are you going to the butte?" Matt Two Bull asked.

"Later. I gotta take the rocks I got yesterday to the
trader first. He's paying me two dollars for a small bag now
and twenty-five cents up to fifty cents for the big agates."

"That is good," answered the old man.

"Well, it's about time he started paying me," Norman
said. "That tightwad has been cheating me all these years.
You know what I'm going to do with the money, Grandpa?
I'm going to save it to buy a rifle and rock polishing equipment like the trader's."

Norman stood as if sighting a rifle at a deer, "I'll get me
a big buck this fall. Maybe two. I'll send venison for you to
eat when you're at Aunt Martha's this winter and save the
hides for you."

"*Waśte*, good." Matt Two Bull was pleased. "What will
you do with the polishing machine?"

"I'm going to have my own business. Sell agates right to
the tourists and show that old Brannon that he can't hold
down a smart Indian. I'm going to make lots of money and
put that crook out of business." Norman got excited as he
spoke of his plans. "I'll make so much money that I'll chase
all the white men off the reservation. I'll make us rich,
Grandpa!"

But Matt Two Bull was looking sadly at Norman.
"You are talking like a white man," he softly reprimanded.
"Being rich isn't important to an Indian."

"Well, it ought to be," Norman said. "It's beca
dians don't have money that the whites have taken
everything."

"You want to be like a white man?" Matt Two B.
asked gently. "Do you think all will be good then?"

"Why not?"

"Your mother has accepted the white man's church and
you've seen how she's changed. Don't you think having lots
of money like the white men will change you too?"

Norman didn't answer.

"Think of the *coup* stick you found. It was used to show
that a man had courage to do a dangerous thing and killing
was not important. Today we can not do that kind of brave
deed that might cost us our life, but there are some things
that are more important than others."

"What do you mean?" Norman asked.

"You see the way I choose to live?" Matt Two Bull
waved his hand around him at the tent, the clearing, the
clear stream. "I could sell these lands, be a rich man, live in
a house as fancy as a white man's. But I will not. I am an
Indian. Here I am close to the earth to listen," he pointed
to the butte, "for the Thunders' messages from *Wakantanka*."

"But I can't live like this," Norman said.

"No," the old man paused to gather his thoughts. "But
you can still honor the old ways even as you live in the new."

"Do you mean that all of the white man's ways are
bad?" Norman asked.

Matt Two Bull shook his head from side to side. "Sit-ll, one of our old chiefs, told the people, 'When you something good in the white man's road, pick it up. en you find something bad, or that turns out bad, drop it d leave it alone.' "

"You sound like a preacher," Norman said as he turned to leave, and then he remembered why he had come. "I'm supposed to tell you that the minister from Mom's church might be coming to see you. Dad said to tell you to talk to him and explain the old ways. Dad couldn't do it." And then he added thoughtfully, "I guess I can't either."

"You do not understand?" Matt Two Bull asked, and when Norman looked at his grandfather he saw that the old man was hurt.

"No, not really," Norman answered gently, not wanting to wound his grandfather more. "Ever since I found that *coup* stick many strange things have been happening. The stick becomes newer-looking each day and with every change good fortune seems to follow. Like, why did Mr. Brannon all of a sudden start paying me for the agates?" Norman questioned. "Then, too, I'm finding more bigger and better rocks. Dad got a promotion . . ." he stopped with a shrug.

Matt Two Bull nodded and said, "The stick is *Wakan*."

Norman was not satisfied with his grandfather's answer. "But why? How can the stick change when no one has touched it? Why did the good things happen?"

His grandfather shook his head and smiled, "Can't you be content with the knowledge that they have happened?"

Norman, confused and frustrated by his grandfather's answer, left for home.

When Norman walked into the house he fou— mother sitting at the table staring at the *coup* stick. looked too and a tremor of fear went through him.

The changes in the stick up until now had been notic— able, but only as if the leather had been freshened and the colors renewed. Now the short brittle remnants of the leather tie thongs had lengthened and dangled down as if newly placed on the stick.

Sarah jumped up from the table. "I've been waiting for you to come home so that I can leave. I'm not going to stay here alone with that—" Unable to describe it she pointed at the stick. "I'm going to drive into the agency to do our wash and spend the rest of the day with your Aunt Martha. Did Grandpa send his dirty clothes?" she asked as she picked up a basket of laundry.

"No," Norman said. He was so engrossed in examining the *coup* stick that he wasn't paying much attention to what Sarah said.

"Well, I'm going. Why don't you come with me, Nor— man. You haven't been to town since school let out."

"No," Norman said, tearing his eyes away from the stick. "I'll walk over to the trading post with my agates and then go on to the butte."

"Well, be careful, Son. I'll be home in time to fix supper. I'll give you a ride to the store," Sarah offered as she went to the door.

"I'll walk," Norman answered. He wanted to be by himself to think about the stick and what his grandfather had said. He tied the small bag of agates to his belt and threw the sack of bigger rocks over his shoulder, giving one last glance at the *coup* stick as he left the house.

orman walked slowly down the middle of the gravel
. He was unaware of the settling dust in the wake of the
car as his mother drove to the highway. His thoughts
ere in a turmoil, and he didn't notice the larger cloud of
dust as a car approached until a horn blared. He jumped as a
station wagon stopped only a few feet from him.

Norman was surprised to see a big new car on the road.
Few cars such as this one ventured off the paved highway
onto the rough back roads of the reservation. A white man
got out of the car and Norman recognized him as the tourist
who bought his agates yesterday.

"Hello," the man greeted. "Sorry I almost ran you
down. You didn't seem to see me coming."

Norman shook his head, sheepishly shy.

"I was hoping to find you," the man went on. "The
owner of the trading post said he didn't know where you
lived, but I found out at the gas station."

Norman smiled to think that Mr. Brannon didn't want
the tourist to find him.

"I'd like to get some more of those rough agates," the
tourist said.

Wordlessly Norman held out the small bag but didn't
offer the larger one.

"Good," the man said and reached for his wallet. He
gave Norman two dollars. "Say, where do you find these
rocks?"

Norman pointed to the butte looming high in the west.

"That looks like a ways off," the man said. "Is there
a road to it?"

"No," Norman said, finally able to speak desp shyness.

"How do you get there?"

"Walk," answered Norman.

"Whew," the tourist whistled. He gazed thoughtfully at the butte and asked, "Will you take me and my family over there to look for agates?"

Norman stared in surprise at the man's request. Then his eyes went to the man's short pants, bright socks and sandals, and Norman smiled. "That's rough country. It takes almost all day to walk over there and back. There's snakes and rock slides on the butte too."

"You mean I'm not dressed for such a hike?" The man smiled and Norman almost liked him.

Norman nodded and then looked at the car where the woman and two boys sat watching and listening. "It's no place for them either," he said.

"Maybe we're not prepared to go this time, but if I come again I'd like to climb the butte. I've heard that the Thunder Butte is one of the old Sioux holy places," the tourist said as he gazed at the butte. "I'd sure like to look around up there." When he turned back to Norman the white man's pale blue eyes looked shifty and greedy. "I bet there's all kinds of valuable relics buried on the butte," the tourist concluded.

Norman's mouth tightened in anger. This white man felt free to take from the Indians just the way all white people did. "No!" Norman said shortly. "I can't take you up there." He turned and started walking home.

Why not?" the man called after him.

Norman turned. He felt that he had to say something that would conclusively persuade the man from wanting to go to the butte. "The butte *is* a holy place. The Thunders don't like strangers up there."

"Thunders?" questioned the tourist.

"Yes," Norman answered in a solemn voice. "The Thunders live on the butte and send messages from the Great Spirit to the Indians. But they send rock slides to crush those who dare to climb the butte with unholy thoughts." Norman turned and walked away, leaving the tourist standing with his mouth open. He heard the man say something about "superstitious people" to his wife. Then the car door slammed and the tires spun in the gravel as the stranger backed up and drove off the way he had come.

Norman laughed out loud as he watched the dust settle after the receding car. He suddenly felt very good as he realized he believed every word that he had spoken about the butte. His confused thoughts had vanished, leaving him content. He was glad he hadn't shown the tourist the large agates, but he hesitated about taking the rocks to Mr. Brannon. 'No,' he thought. 'I'm not even going to sell them to Mr. Brannon.' He would keep them himself.

When Norman got back to the house he decided he didn't even want to look for more agates. He had a half-formed thought that perhaps the agates should stay on the butte. He vigorously attacked the manure-covered floor of the horse shed, scooping it out and then spreading fresh straw. John Two Bull rarely had time to do this and Nor-

man had been so busy hunting rocks that the shed n
cleaning. He put fresh hay into the mare's manger, dun
the watering trough on his mother's tomato plants and
filled it with fresh well water.

It was long past noon when he finished, and his stomach
was grumbling and complaining. Whistling he walked into
the empty house and made himself a peanut butter sandwich. When he was finished eating he glanced up at the *coup*
stick.

He was not frightened now. "What's going to happen
next?" he asked the stick. He pulled a chair under the window and climbed up to examine the stick. Up close the
leather did not seem so bright and fresh. Curious, Norman
lifted his hands to touch the leather. The chair tipped and he
fell to the floor. His fear returned as he picked himself up.
"So," he said aloud to the stick, "you don't want me to touch
you." He moved the chair back to the table and left the
house.

He got the ax from the shed and started chopping the
logs his father had brought from the creek into stove-size
chunks. He knew this was a job he'd have to do before fall
and thought he might as well begin now.

He chopped until his arms ached. Then he stacked the
wood in neat piles by the shed. He paused once to pump a
cold drink from the well and quit working when the sun
was low.

He was hot, sweaty and weary. He wanted a shower,
but since his house didn't have one he thought a swim in the
creek would do.

Norman headed down to where the beavers had
.med the stream into a small but deep pond. He stripped
. his sweat-damp clothes and dived into the water. He
wam across the pond and then floated on his back. Dreamily
he watched the slow-drifting clouds in the blue sky and was
content. He closed his eyes and then quickly opened them
when he felt water splashing on his face.

In his surprise his head went under, and as he came
sputtering to the surface he heard the deep laughter of his
grandfather.

"Ho, Grandpa," Norman called to the old man squat-
ting on the bank, "you want a water fight?"

Matt Two Bull backed off. "No," he said as if in fright,
"I do not."

Norman splashed out of the water, shook the excess
moisture from his hair and body and dressed. The sun was
behind the butte now and the air in the shade was chilly.
Norman shivered as he squatted near his grandfather.

"Why didn't you go to the butte today?" Matt Two
Bull asked.

"I don't know," Norman replied as he listlessly began
tossing twigs into the creek. "I didn't feel like it after I talked
to that white tourist who bought my rocks." He explained
what had happened.

"So I went home, cleaned the horse shed, chopped wood
and came swimming. I guess I didn't want to stay in the
house with the *coup* stick. It's spooky, Grandpa."

"But there is nothing to be afraid of," the old man said
calmly. He stood and said, "You had better go home. The
sun is down and your father and mother will be home. They

think you went to the butte and if you are not home they will think you are lying hurt up there."

"Yeah," Norman agreed, getting to his feet. "Why do you come for supper, Grandpa? Mom will probably bring some good meat from town."

"No," the old man turned to walk upstream to his tent, "not tonight. I will see you in the morning."

VI

COUP FEATHER

When Norman entered the house he saw that his father stood looking up at the *coup* stick. Sarah was scolding as she prepared supper. "You may say that thing up there is nothing to be afraid of, but I don't like it. Maybe the good things which have happened to us since Norman brought it home have come to us because we work hard and live right. Have you ever thought of that? That stick might not have anything to do with it at all."

John ignored her and turned smiling to Norman. "I see you had a busy day. The old mare is happy with her clean stall, and the wood pile looks like you got a good start on the winter stack." He sat down at the table. "Did you sell your agates to Mr. Brannon?"

Norman shook his head and joined his father at the table. "No, that white tourist came out here to see me. I met

him on the road and sold him the small bag of rocks. I k
the big ones."

"The trader isn't going to be happy about your selling
the rocks to the tourist when you said you'd take more to
the trading post," John said.

Norman shrugged, "I don't care."

"You shouldn't go back on your word, Norman," Sarah
said as she served supper.

"I didn't promise I'd take the rocks to him," Norman
protested.

Soon after supper a car drove into the yard and the family was surprised to see that their visitor was Mr. Brannon.

The trader had never been to the Two Bulls' home before and Norman knew the man had come because he must
have heard about Norman's selling the agates to the tourist.
Norman stood stiffly beside his father and prepared to defend
himself.

But the trader greeted the family pleasantly. "Nice
evening. Yes, don't mind if I do," he said in answer to
Sarah's offer of coffee.

The man sipped the brew, and the family sat quietly
waiting for him to reveal the purpose of his visit. Finally
Mr. Brannon cleared his throat and spoke. "Norman, I heard
at the gas station about that tourist coming to see you and
how he talked you into selling your agates to him." He shook
his head sorrowfully. "Now, you haven't had any experience
dealing with tourists and you gotta be careful. They're out
to cheat you." He took a drink of coffee, and Norman
glanced at his father, who was smiling at the thought of the
trader worrying about Norman being cheated.

"I also heard that that tourist has been asking around ying to find someone to take him up to the butte so that ıe can snoop out relics," the trader went on.

"Yeah," Norman agreed, "he wanted me to take him."

"Well, I hope you didn't say you would?" Norman shook his head and the trader continued. "Well, I got suspicious as to the man's reasons for wanting to go to the butte and got to thinking." He paused for another sip.

"Now, lately I know you've been finding more and bigger agates up on that hill than you ever have before, right?"

"Since I've been searching on the west slope where there's lots of loose rock," Norman explained, "the agates are easier to find."

"Well, it seems to me," Mr. Brannon said slowly, "that there may be more agates on the butte than either of us realize. I mean more than just the few I need to sell to the tourists. I'm wondering if that butte and the surrounding area might not be a large natural deposit that could be developed into a small business for this reservation."

"What do you mean?" John asked.

"Agates are used for other things besides just as pretty stones for jewelry," the trader explained. "Some industries use them. The larger stones can be made into vases, dishes, ash trays and other decorative items."

"What are you thinking about doing?" John asked.

"I wonder if you could get the tribal council to hire a man who's an expert on that kind of thing, to come out and survey the area to see if a quarry operation would be possible and worthwhile."

"If such a thing came about," John seemed to be think-

ing aloud, "it could mean jobs for the people." The tr㬘
nodded in agreement. "But," John asked, "what do you w㬘
out of it?"

"Well, now, John," the trader laughed, "I guess you
know me pretty good to understand that even if I couldn't
profit directly from a quarry, I sure would indirectly. The
Indians would have more money to spend at my place. Why,
I might even be able to expand, because such an operation
would naturally bring in more business."

Norman had been thinking while the men talked and
now he said, "If I remember from stuff in school—in order
to have a quarry won't the butte have to be dug out and
won't there just be a big hole in the ground left?"

"Now, I ain't no expert on such things. But what if it
did?" Mr. Brannon answered. "That old hill out there ain't
doing any good just standing there being struck by lightning
every time it storms."

"The thunder and lightning is what loosened the rocks
so that I could find the agates," Norman said.

The trader laughed. "Don't tell me that an up-and-com-
ing young man like you believes in that old stuff about the
butte being the home of the thunders? Weren't you the boy
who wanted to get some lapidary equipment so that you
could compete with me? A quarry on that butte would
bring you more money than selling piddly, polished stones
would."

"Grandpa wouldn't like the butte destroyed and neither
would a lot of other Indians."

"Well, now," the trader temporized, "maybe we're
talking too far in the future. Why don't we just get that ex-

out here to investigate all the angles." He held out his
p for a refill from Sarah and saw the *coup* stick hanging
ver the window.

Norman watched the trader's mouth gape and his eyes
pop in covetous longing.

"Where'd you get the *coup* stick?" Mr. Brannon asked.

"Norman found it buried on the butte," John explained.
"It is very old."

Mr. Brannon nodded. "Don't find many of those around
anymore. It looks like it's in good shape." He paused as if
thinking. "Want to sell it?"

John looked at Norman, but it was Sarah who answered, "How much will you give for it?"

"Fifty bucks," the trader said.

Norman gasped at the sum. He knew that Indian relics
were valuable, but he was still surprised at the offer. He
looked at the stick and suddenly it was only a brittle length
of wood covered with rotten leather. He wondered how the
stock looked to the trader. He turned to see if his father had
noticed and was shocked to hear his father bargaining.

"Seventy dollars," John said.

Norman saw a bit of leather flake off the stick. "No!"
he cried. "The *coup* stick is not for sale!"

His parents turned to Norman in amazed shock. "Norman," Sarah cried, "what do you mean, not for sale?"

John was looking up at the stick and Sarah followed his
glance. Her eyes widened as she too saw the change. The
trader looked too, but if he noticed anything he did not say.

Norman's father gave a deep sigh. "My son is right," he
said sadly. "Sarah has been wanting the stick out of the house

and I thought selling it would do the trick. In my greed I forgot that the stick is *Wakan*. We cannot sell it.

Norman looked at his mother, who had her hand over her mouth. There were tears in her eyes. She nodded in agreement, "It's not for sale."

"What do you mean, *Wakan*?" the trader asked angrily. "It's just an old relic the boy found. You think it's got some special power?"

John nodded. "Unusually good things have happened to us since the stick has been in our house. If we sell it—well, bad things might happen."

"Bah!" exclaimed Mr. Brannon scornfully. "You Indians are just a bunch of superstitious heathens. I'm surprised at you, Mrs. Two Bull. You belong to the church and should know better," he said to Sarah, who shook her head and turned away.

The trader stood. "No wonder you people never get ahead in this world. It ain't civilized to believe in that *Wakan* stuff!" He walked to the door and then turned.

"Even if you won't sell the stick, don't forget to talk to the council about that agate quarry," he said to John as he left.

Norman looked at his father and mother. John was looking at the floor, and Sarah was weeping softly. Norman looked away and up at the *coup* stick. "Look!" he cried.

The *coup* stick was again glowing with bright colors, and now a single eagle feather hung from the staff.

VII

BACK TO THE EARTH

The sun had not risen when Norman was awakened by his father's gentle shake.

"Get up, Son," John said quietly. "There is something we must do before I go to work."

Norman dressed quickly and walked into the lamp-lit room. His father motioned to where the *coup* stick hung.

The eagle feather was gone, the colors faded and lifeless.

"Take it down," John said, and Norman pulled a chair up to the window. He did not fall this time, and he found the leather brittle in his hands as he lifted the stick.

Matt Two Bull was waiting as they reached the creek and wordlessly he joined the small procession.

They stopped at the base of the butte, and as the sun began to rise they gave the *coup* stick back to the earth.